SCHOLASTIC INC.
New York Toronto London Auckland
Sydney Mexico City New Delhi Hong Kong

Duck! Rabbit!

AMY KROUSE ROSENTHAL & TOM LICHTENHELD

Hey, look! A duck!

That's not a duck.
That's a rabbit!

Are you kidding me?
It's totally a duck.

See, there's his bill.

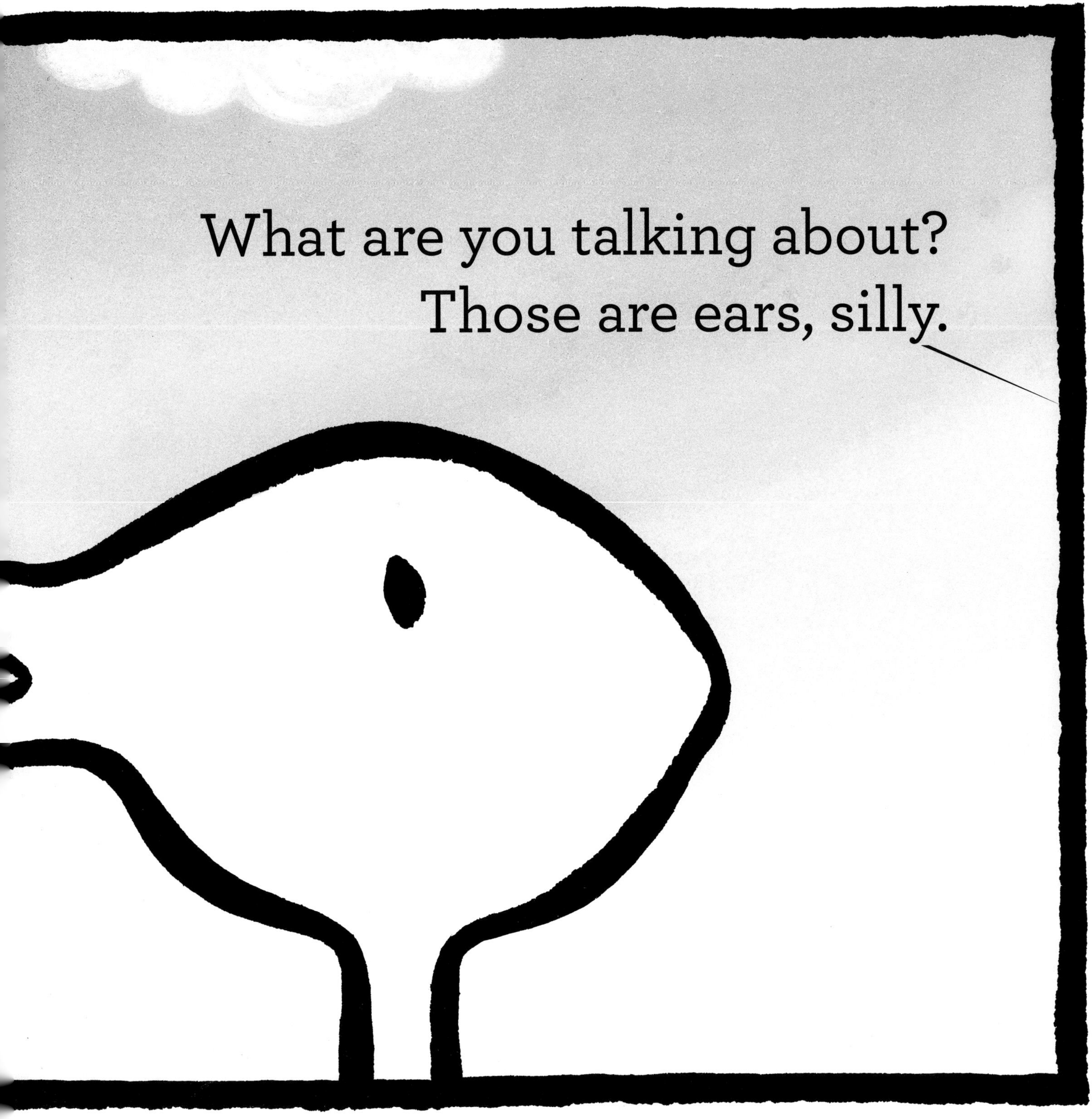
What are you talking about?
Those are ears, silly.

It's a duck. And he's about
to eat a piece of bread.

It's a rabbit. And he's about to eat a carrot.

Wait. Listen. Did you hear that?
I heard duck sounds.

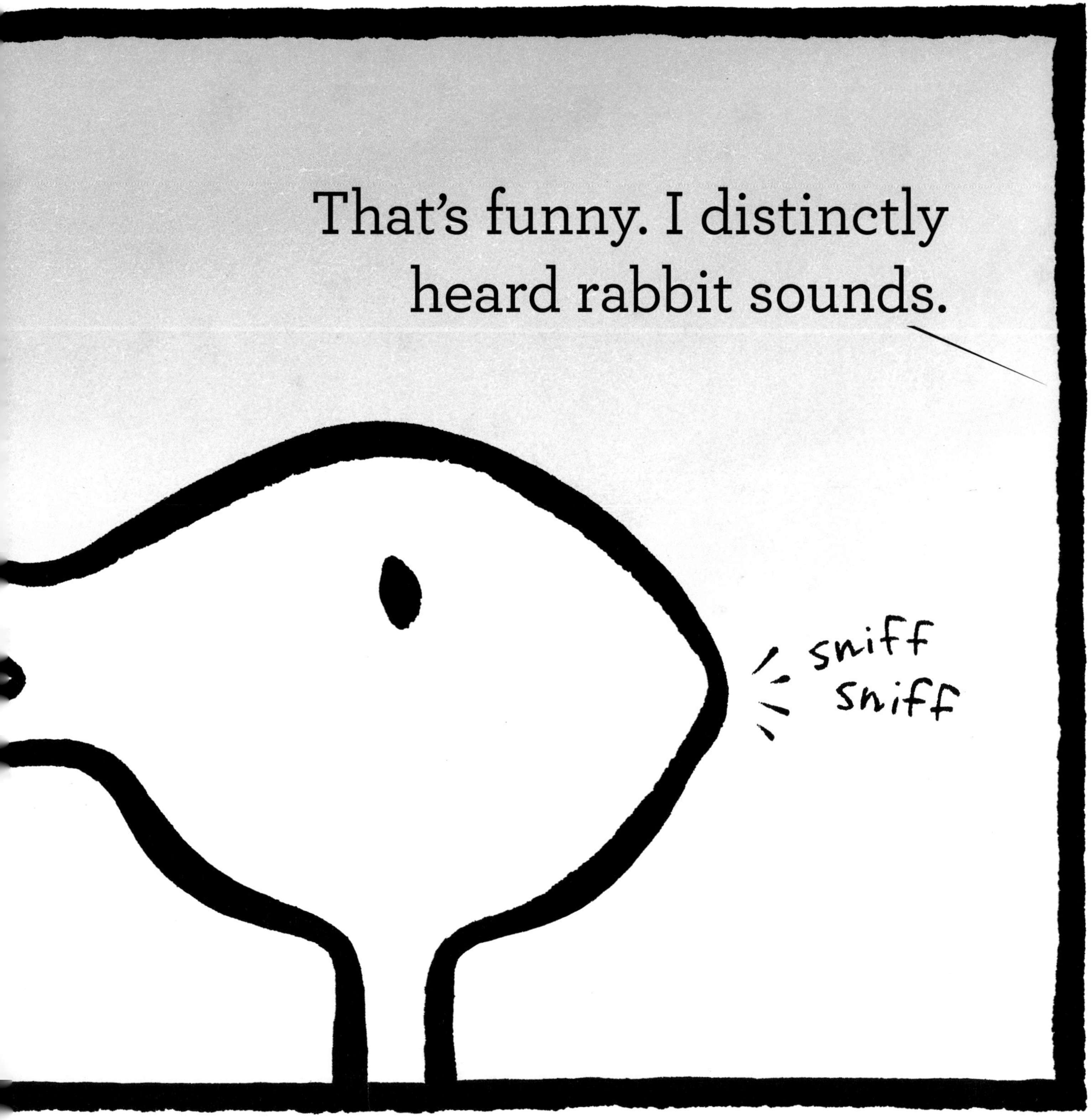
That's funny. I distinctly heard rabbit sounds.
sniff sniff

Now the duck is wading through the swamp.

No, the rabbit is hiding in the grass.

There, see? It's flying!

Flying? It's hopping!

Look, the
duck is so hot,
he's getting
a drink.

Here,
look at
the duck
through my
binoculars.

Sorry,
still a
rabbit.

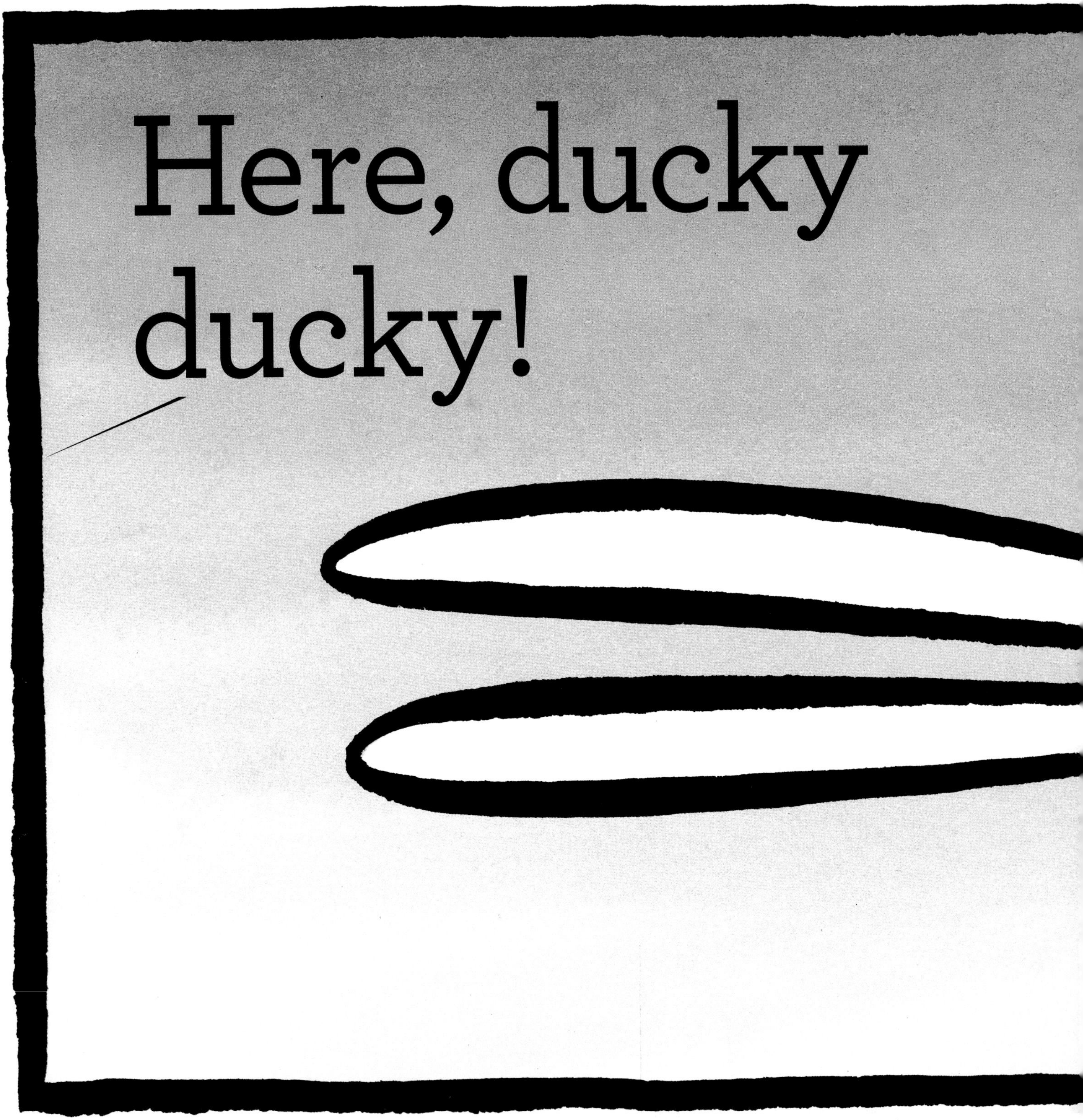
Here, ducky ducky!

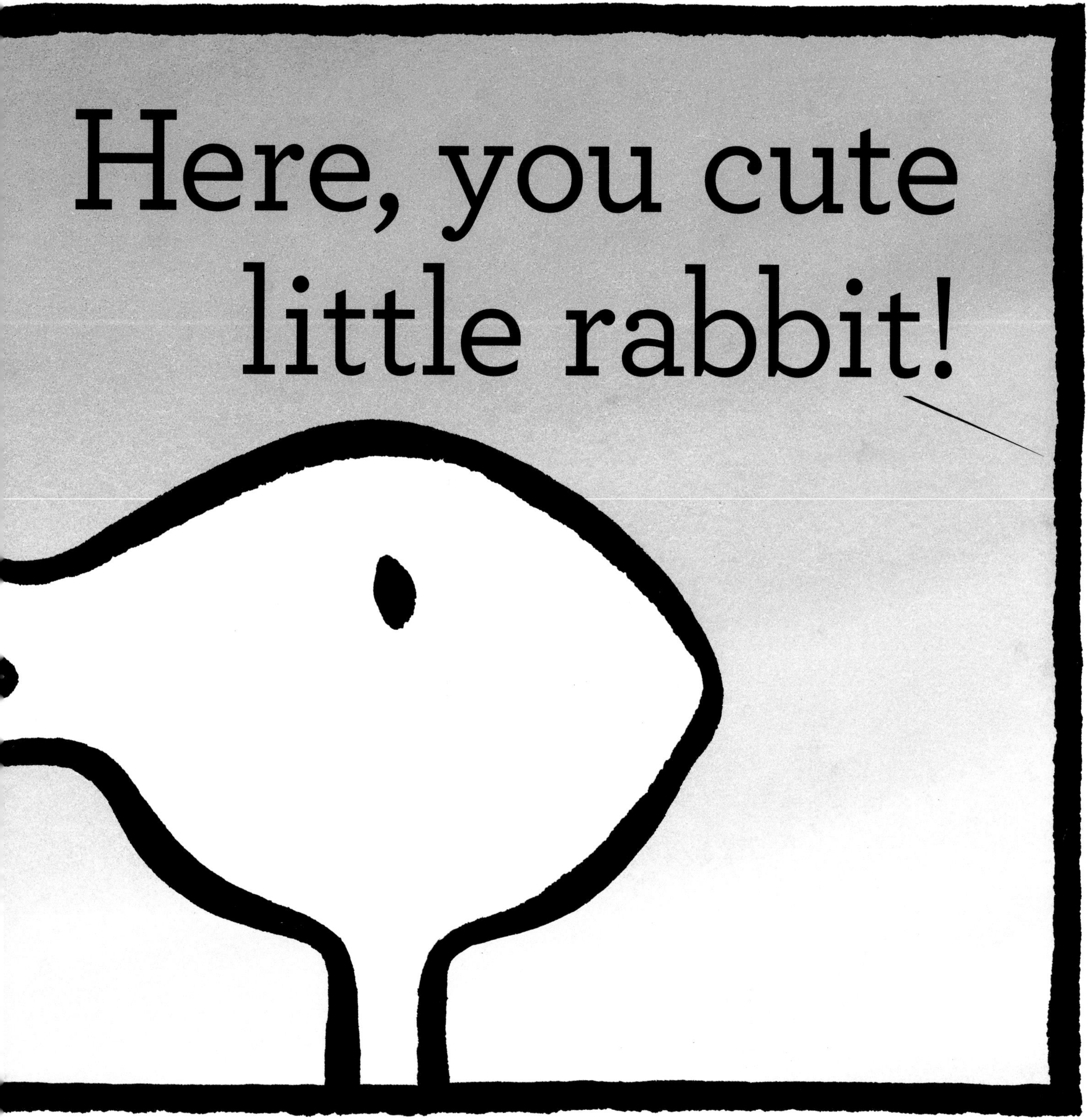
Here, you cute little rabbit!

Oh great, you scared him away.

I didn't scare him away.
You scared him away.

You know, maybe you were right.
Maybe it *was* a rabbit.

Thing is, now I'm actually thinking it was a duck.

Well, anyway...now what
do you want to do?

I don't know. What do *you* want to do?

Hey, look! An anteater!

That's no anteater.
That's a brachiosaurus!

The End.

(It's not the end! There's still all this stuff!)

Thanks to Jan for her unwavering support.
Thanks to Eric Rohmann and Larry Day for their artful camaraderie. —T. L.

Duck . . . duck . . . duck . . . GOOSE! I pick Charise Mericle Harper. —A. K. R.

And thanks to Marshall Ross for putting us in the same room. —T. L. and A. K. R.

ISBN 978-0-545-25792-3

12 11 10 9 8 7 6 5 4 3 2 1   10 11 12 13 14 15/0

Printed in Mexico   49

First Scholastic printing, April 2010

Book design by Tom Lichtenheld and Kristine Brogno
Typeset in Archer
The illustrations were rendered in ink, watercolor, and a wee bit of colored pencil.